THE SECRETS OF DROON

— TONY ABBOTT —

Escape from Jabar-Loo

Illustrated by David Merrell
Cover illustration by Tim Jessell

A
LITTLE APPLE
PAPERBACK

SCHOLASTIC INC.
New York Toronto London Auckland Sydney
Mexico City New Delhi Hong Kong Buenos Aires

To Janie and Lucy, always

For more information about the continuing saga of Droon,
please visit Tony Abbott's website at
www.tonyabbottbooks.com

ISBN-13: 978-0-439-90251-9
ISBN-10: 0-439-90251-7

Text copyright © 2007 by Tony Abbott.
Illustrations copyright © 2007 by Scholastic Inc.

All rights reserved. Published by Scholastic Inc.
SCHOLASTIC, LITTLE APPLE, and associated logos
are trademarks and/or registered trademarks of Scholastic Inc.

12 11 10 9 8 7 6 5 4 3   9 10 11 12/0

Printed in the U.S.A.
First printing, June 2007

Contents

One

Three Heads Are Better

"*Habba . . . habbza . . . snkk . . . snkk!*"

Eric Hinkle woke up with a start and blinked his eyes open. "Mom? Dad?"

No one answered.

Then he saw the poster of "Sandwiches of the World" on the wall, and he remembered he wasn't in his own bedroom. He was sleeping at his friend Neal's house.

And Neal was snoring — *snkk!* — again.

"Wake up, Noisy Nose," said Eric. "I

need to know if you dreamed about Droon last night."

Neal sat up in bed, then flopped back down. "Huh? Yeah. What? *Snkk* . . ."

"Neal," said Eric. "Your dreams. Droon!"

Droon, of course, was the magical world Eric, Neal, and their friend Julie had discovered under Eric's basement.

It was a land of close friends, mysterious places, and dangerous enemies. It was a place of adventure and excitement.

One of the best things about Droon was that Eric, Neal, and Julie had developed powers there.

Magical powers!

Eric sat up in his sleeping bag and gently flicked his fingers. *Zzzt!* He smiled as they sent off a tiny spray of silver sparks. He loved his magical abilities. He couldn't ever imagine being without them. Besides being able to shoot sparks, he had visions.

He could also create charms and read old languages. He was becoming as powerful as his friend Princess Keeah. Maybe even more powerful!

His friend Julie could change her shape and had developed the ability to fly. She could also fly others around with her. Neal had recently been revealed as Zabilac, a time-traveling genie with quirky powers.

All that was amazing and wonderful and fun. But there was another reason Eric couldn't wait to return to Droon.

"Neal," he said. "Wake up!"

His friend yawned loudly. "Dude, it's tough to remember stuff when your brain won't wake up until your stomach does."

"Well, wake up your stomach," said Eric. "We need to get to Droon as soon as we can."

Looking out Neal's window, he saw the

sun slanting across his house two streets away. His heart beat faster when he saw the apple trees in his yard.

Apples, he thought. *They're the reason I need to get back to Droon!*

In a recent vision, a strange figure had appeared to Eric. It was hidden in green mist and smelled of apples. Its voice — which he did not recognize — warned him that Droon's wizards would face a mysterious challenge.

Eric wasn't sure, but he felt that because the figure had appeared only to him, it might have been a special message just for him. After all, apples were unknown in Droon, and he was the only one of his friends who had apple trees in his yard.

What he *did* know was what Keeah had told them all. The green mist meant that the figure had just returned from Droon's future.

The future!

Ever since then, Eric had tried to think of who besides genies could travel in time.

Only one name came to mind.

Salamandra, the Thorn Princess of Pesh.

Eric shuddered when he remembered her. Salamandra was a mysterious princess from his world who traveled through time in her city of Pesh. When Pesh was sent back to the ancient world, Salamandra fled into Droon, where she had immediately begun making mischief.

But no sooner had Eric thought of Salamandra than he dismissed the idea. The last time the kids had seen her, she was following Emperor Ko, the dreaded ruler of beasts. And Ko was all about the past, not the future.

So who? he wondered. *Who could it be?*

But if Eric didn't know exactly who it

might be, he was certain that the scent of apples meant something important.

Something . . . *special* . . . just for him.

If I go to Droon, I can find out! he thought.

But going to Droon was tricky. There were only two ways to get there. If he, Neal, or Julie dreamed about Droon, it meant that Keeah or the wizard Galen was calling them.

The other way to get there was if their magic soccer ball brought them a message.

But Eric had not dreamed of Droon since their last visit there. And the soccer ball was locked safely inside his house.

"So, Neal. What did you dream about?"

Neal sighed. "Mostly peanut butter," he said. "But there were meatballs, too.

And celery. That's almost like health food, isn't it?"

Eric rolled his eyes. "Meatballs? Peanut butter? Neal, you're weird."

"Thanks," he said. "It's what makes me special."

Eric frowned when he heard the word *special*. He flopped back into his sleeping bag. "Well, we need to go back. So much is happening."

"No kidding," Neal agreed. "We have to rescue Keeah's parents, for one thing."

Eric was startled to realize that he had nearly forgotten about that. "Of course! That's what I mean. We have to get them home safely."

Keeah's parents, King Zello and Queen Relna, along with the whole royal navy, had recently been shipwrecked by storms in a mysterious and distant land called

Jabar-Loo. At the end of their last visit to Droon, Keeah had been preparing to go there in search of them.

Eric got up. "Maybe Julie had a dream —"

Suddenly, Neal clamped his hand on Eric's mouth. "*Shh!* I hear footsteps."

Reaching under his pillow, Neal pulled out a small square of blue cloth. He gave it a snap. *Floop!* The cloth unfolded itself into an object the size of an umbrella.

It was his genie turban.

Neal crept across the floor and tilted his head, as if the turban were helping him hear. "It's too early for Mom to be awake. . . . It must be . . ."

Eric froze. "Holy cow . . . what?"

"A thief!" said Neal. "It *is* a thief! My genie ears tell me. He's stealing something round . . . flat . . ."

"What could it be?" asked Eric.

"MY PANCAKES!" Neal shouted.

Eric blinked. "What?"

"Dad is stealing my pancakes!" cried Neal. He stuffed his turban into his pajama top and tore down the stairs, screaming, "Stop, thief!"

Eric stared at the open door for a second, then sighed. "Some adventure. Some mystery. Meatballs. Pancakes."

He gazed through the window at the apple trees, which were now turning gold in the morning sunlight.

"So who would come *only* to me and tell me stuff?" he asked himself. "And was there more they wanted to tell me?"

A moment later, Neal was back in the room, licking an empty plate, his turban low on his brow. "I was totally right. Dad ate all my pancakes. Luckily, I used my genie powers, went into the past, and saved them. I saved yours, too."

Eric looked at the empty plate. "You saved mine? Then where are they?"

Neal licked syrup from his fingers. "I got hungry on the way upstairs."

"Neal —!" cried Eric.

"But guess what," his friend said. "When I let Snorky out, I found this on the back step."

He lifted his turban, and the magic soccer ball dropped into his hand.

"What?" said Eric. "That ball was locked in my basement." He took the ball and examined it closely. "But there's no message —"

All of a sudden — *whammm!* — the soccer ball flew out of his hands and smacked him hard on the forehead.

"Whoa, direct hit!" Neal said, laughing. Then he blinked. "Eric, that ball totally put letters on your head. They spell . . . *anso* . . ."

Eric stared at him. "The ball always

spells things backward. So *anso* means . . .
osna. But letters printed on my head are
probably backward anyway so it really
is *anso*."

"What's *anso*?" asked Neal.

Eric shrugged. "I never heard of *anso* —"

Just then, the ball smacked Neal in the
head. Twice.

Eric nearly fell down laughing.

"Double direct hit!" he said. "The letters
on your head say . . . *asis*. So that's . . .
asis . . . *anso*. It still doesn't make sense —"

Suddenly — *boing!* — the ball flew like
a rocket out the open window.

Neal jumped. "Holy cow. I bet it's going
to hit Julie's head now! I have to see this!"

The boys dressed in seconds, then ran
out of Neal's house and across his backyard
to the corner. Pausing to make sure no traf-
fic was coming, they dashed across the
street to Julie's house and rang the bell.

Julie opened the door, holding her head. "You guys will never believe —"

"*Kh*," said Neal.

Julie frowned. "Excuse me?"

"Your forehead says *kh*!" said Neal.

"The ball hit us, too," said Eric. "We think there's a message spelled out on our foreheads. Come to my house, quick!"

Five minutes later, the three friends were crowded in Eric's bathroom, staring at their faces in the mirror.

Standing first in one order, then another, and turning the letters around once more, they finally deciphered the ball's message.

Khan's oasis

"Khan's oasis in Lumpland!" said Julie. "We're being called to Droon!"

"To rescue Keeah's parents," said Neal.

And learn more about my vision! thought Eric.

The three friends rushed down the basement stairs, cleared some boxes away from a door under the stairs, and entered a tiny closet.

The moment they switched off the ceiling light — *whoosh!* — the cement floor vanished, and in its place appeared the top step of a long, curving staircase. The staircase to Droon.

Julie leaned down, trying to see beyond the clouds below. "The air is sweet. I'd know that smell anywhere. It's the desert."

One by one, the three friends ran down the stairs. Passing through the clouds, they saw vast seas of sand sparkling in the pink air of dawn. Near the bottom of the stairs stood a ring of tall dunes surrounded by palm trees.

"I do like a door-to-door staircase," said

Neal. "This is Khan's oasis, all right. Keeah must be in there. Let's hike over the dunes."

But no sooner had they begun to climb the sand than — *whoomf!* — Neal fell to the ground as if his legs were pulled out from under him. "Hey!"

Not a second later, Julie was facedown in the sand. "Who did that —?"

Before he could run, Eric, too, fell to the ground in a tangled heap. "Stop —!"

Over and over the three friends tumbled, all the way down to the bottom of the dune!

Two

Doing the Wave

"Hel-lel-lelllppp!" cried Neal.

"Oh, please hush," hissed a tiny voice when they had all stopped rolling.

Looking up, they beheld a purple creature the size and shape of a sofa pillow. He had a crown on his head and tassels dangling from his shoulders. His hands were perched on his pillowy hips, and he was chuckling at them.

"Khan!" said Julie. "That was you?"

Khan was the king of the purple Lumpies of Lumpland and the kids' long-time friend. He adjusted his crown and straightened his tassels. "And not a moment too soon, either."

"But Keeah called us here," said Neal. "Why did you tackle us?"

"Simple, my friends," he said. "It was not Keeah who called you, but I. And if you follow me, I'll show you why!"

Khan led the children step by step up the side of the giant dune. Peeping carefully over the top, they spied a pool of blue water. Princess Keeah stood in a small boat at its center. Her long blond hair was tied in braids, her hands were folded, and her eyes were shut tight.

"What is she doing?" Julie whispered. "She looks as if she's in a trance."

"Nearly," said the Lumpy king. "Keeah is in the middle of a very tricky charm. If you disturb her, you'll spoil it —"

"Like Daddy did," said a tiny voice.

"Twice!" said another tiny voice.

Two smaller pillows, one with pink tassels, the other with blue, scrambled out from behind a palm tree, giggling. They were followed by a third, larger Lumpy, wearing a crown like Khan's.

The king glared at the two smaller pillows, then smiled. "Meet my children, Sasha and Lena. And Mrs. Khan, of course, my queen."

The friends bowed to the Lumpy queen, and she to them. "Keeah is conjuring a very difficult charm to help find her parents," she said. "She hasn't had much luck so far —"

All of a sudden, the water in the pool began to churn wildly.

"Yes!" Keeah called out. "It's coming!"

But no sooner had the princess spoken than the water stopped and went still again.

"Oh, pooh! This isn't working at all!" Keeah said. When she saw her friends, she waved and paddled quickly to shore.

"Thank you for coming!" she said. "Only a very tricky spell will take us to my parents. But without Galen, I can't get it right."

"Where is he?" asked Eric.

Keeah shared a serious look with the Lumpy king. "Things have changed since we last saw you."

"Tell us everything," said Julie.

Keeah led them all to the Khans' purple tent on the far side of the oasis.

"We know that my parents were marooned in the distant land of Jabar-Loo," she said as they entered the tent. "Galen sent his messenger Flink to help them, but Flink never found them. Galen guessed something was wrong, so he and Max went at once."

"Being a spider troll, Max is quite good at finding people," said Khan. "Take it from an expert tracker!"

Keeah nodded. "But we've had no word from them, either."

Khan unrolled a map on the floor of the tent. "Jabar-Loo has ever been a land of mystery. It remains so. Look."

At the very eastern edges of Droon sat the western shore of a vast, featureless land. Its interior was dark and unmarked.

"As you see, we know next to nothing about Jabar-Loo," said Keeah. "Few explorers have ever been to its forest. But there are tales of strange enchantments."

The children looked at one another.

"Enchantments?" said Julie.

"You may remember that mischievous mask maker, Hob," said Khan, shaking his head in disapproval. "Hob learned dark magic from the temples there!"

Hob! thought Eric excitedly. The last time they had seen the little imp, he had run off with Salamandra's magic staff.

Could Salamandra be involved in this, after all? Eric wondered. *Could she possibly be the one who appeared to me in my vision?*

Mrs. Khan hugged her children and placed her hands over their ears. "The old temples of Goll lie in ruins among the trees," she whispered. "There are legends of giant rats crawling among the forest stones, and wild beasts, and shadows cast by nothing! Time itself is said to flow topsy-turvy in Jabar-Loo."

Neal straightened the turban on his

head. "It sounds like whoever gets lost there needs our help. I'm ready!"

"They say the forest is alive!" said Lena, wiggling out from her mother's hug.

"There's black fog, too," added Sasha. "And strange noises. And music —"

"Children, hush," Mrs. Khan scolded. "Your father is going there, you know!"

The two smaller Lumpies looked at each other with astonishment, then turned to their father, their tiny chins quivering.

"Oh, now, little ones," said Khan soothingly. "Come help Papa load Keeah's boat!"

While the Lumpies scampered out of the tent, Keeah continued her tale. "Before he left, Galen asked us to join him on the edge of Jabar-Loo. That's where we're going now."

Julie traced her fingers on the map. "We must be thousands of miles away!"

Keeah winked and led everyone out of

the tent. "That's where my charm comes in. For the quickest way to Jabar-Loo is to conjure the same wave that marooned my parents there. Khan, is everything ready?"

"Ready and waiting!" the king replied.

"We even packed pretzels," said Sasha.

"Really? How many?" asked Neal. "No, wait. Don't tell me. I like surprises."

Eric remembered his vision again. Maybe today would mean more than a simple rescue, after all. Maybe today would be special just for him. Flicking his fingers and watching their tips sizzle, he smiled. "I've got my supplies. Let's do this."

Keeah tiptoed to the shore. She gazed at the center of the pond and spread out her arms, murmuring to herself.

Mrs. Khan hugged her husband tightly. "Remember what they say, dear, and prove them wrong!"

Neal gulped. "What do they say?"

"Few travelers find Jabar-Loo," she said. "Fewer enter. But almost none return!"

Neal shuddered. "*That's* what they say?"

"They do, but pish, posh!" said Khan, tugging his corners nervously. "That's about travelers. But we aren't travelers!"

"We're not?" asked Julie.

"No . . . we're . . . *rescuers*," said the little king. "That's right. We're rescuers, rescuing the king and queen of Droon!"

"Yay, Daddy!" the two smaller Lumpies cried together. "The Hero of Lumpland!"

A spray of water shot up from the center of the pond.

"It's working!" said Keeah. "The magic wave is coming! Everyone in the boat!"

The five friends jumped into the boat and paddled to the center of the pond.

Keeah gave one final shout — "*Mah-toth-malempa, Jabar-Loo!*" — and a giant wave erupted from the water. It shot up

like an enormous fountain and hurled the tiny boat up through the air like a rocket.

Whooooosh! It soared higher and farther and faster over Droon than the children had ever gone before. Below them passed the plains, mountains, and cities of Droon. Just when they saw a vast, dark forest in the distance, the wave fell back to earth, and the tiny boat began to fall.

"Oh, no!" cried Julie. "Hold on tight!"

The friends clung to one another as the boat dropped through the air like a stone.

THWUMP! The boat struck the earth with a terrifying shudder. It skidded across the ground, bounced, flipped five times, rolled over, crunched, cracked, broke apart, and finally plunged hundreds of feet down a bottomless chasm, vanishing out of sight.

Three

The Sound of Music

"Good thing we weren't in that boat," said Julie, peering into the black chasm.

"I've been thinking that, too," said Eric.

"We're all agreed, then," said Keeah.

Seconds before the boat fell apart, its five passengers were thrown onto a patch of tall, soft grass. They now stood at the chasm's edge, staring down.

"Good-bye, pretzels," whispered Neal.

Together, they stepped away from the

edge and faced the most enormous forest they had ever seen. Dark and dense, drifting with mist as thick as night, the forest loomed over them like a living presence.

Eric remembered Mrs. Khan's words.

Few travelers find Jabar-Loo. Fewer enter. But almost none return.

Yet, what if there was a secret inside meant only for him? He knew he had to keep going, no matter what.

Just then a sound fell over them that was neither wind in the trees, nor the chirping of birds, nor their own breathing.

Ooo-la-looooo!

"What *is* that?" whispered Julie as the sound coiled and echoed about the trees.

"Someone is singing," said Keeah. "And I think the song is coming from up there." She pointed at a gnarly tower growing on the edge of the forest like a tree of stone.

But if it were stone, that was not its strangest feature, for the tower's summit looked like nothing so much as the top of a huge muffin.

"I suddenly feel hungry," said Neal.

Ooo-la-looo-looo! Ooo-looo! The song went on for a minute or two, then seemed to cease. But before its echoes faded, the tune began again in the distance. Minutes later, it sounded from still farther away.

"I know what this is," whispered Keeah. "It's a song tower. A *droomar* elf is singing from the top."

The *droomar* were an ancient race of elves that had long worked for the peace of Droon.

"A magical charm is sung in one tower," Keeah said. "It's heard in a nearby tower, whose singer then takes up the song, and so on. The song is passed along for miles without ceasing. Since it never stops, the charm has the power to prevent terrible things from happening."

Eric glanced up at the sides of the tower but saw no openings except at the top. "Maybe if we get inside, the singer can tell us if he saw our friends."

"I'll fly us all up," said Julie. "Everyone take my hands and hold tight."

They did as she said, and Julie leaped from the ground, tugging her friends with her, and flew them all to the tower's top.

Alighting on a windowsill, they looked inside to see an old furry elf. His large cloak trailed to the floor, and he wore a wide, slouchy hat. He stood near a music stand, mumbling to himself. "Me, me, me . . . oh!"

He jumped when he saw the children. "The princess of Droon and her companions! You've come to find the king and queen! Galen and Max, too! Come in!"

The children entered the muffin-shaped chamber and quickly told the little old elf everything that had happened.

"Lost in Jabar-Loo. Yes, yes," he said. "Long ago, it was an outpost of Goll, Emperor Ko's dark land of magic, you know."

"We have a map to prove its darkness," said Khan, tapping his rolled-up scroll.

"Indeed," said the elf. "When Galen defeated Ko, Jabar-Loo's temples fell asleep with the rest of Goll. But lately . . ."

"What?" asked Keeah.

The *droomar* sighed. "For some time, my brothers and I have suspected that something new has woken in Jabar-Loo's enchanted old temples. We believe that, if not for our songs, the dark forest would overrun Droon like a jungle gone wild. Excuse me!"

For a full five minutes the elf sang his part again, then the melody moved on once more.

Eric smiled. "It's beautiful. *Ooo-la-looo!*"

The *droomar* blinked. "Beautifully sung, my boy. You're quite a natural musician. If you ever need a job, do stop by!"

Keeah had been looking out the window at the forest below. She turned. "That old dark magic has somehow trapped my parents and friends inside. We must enter Jabar-Loo now."

The elf nodded. "Then I shall help make your journey a bit easier!"

While he hustled about, the children gazed down at the forest.

"I don't like this at all," said Eric. "No one can tell us exactly what's going on in there, but everyone seems to think it's something scary. It's like . . ."

"Fearing the unknown?" said Khan. "I know I do. Those evil enchantments we have heard of await our arrival."

"And my tuskadons await your arrival, also!" said the *droomar.* "They'll help you travel quickly. Let's go down below. Come."

Five enormous beasts were huffing loudly outside the tower when the children and Khan reached the bottom. They had furry trunks and coiled tusks of blazing scarlet. Each ear was as large as a sail and bore three points, like a bat wing.

"Tuskadons," said Julie. "I like them."

The elf held out an object to them. "Since music helps against dark spells, take this, too. It is the only splangle in all of Droon!"

Eric guessed why. He suspected a splangle was a musical instrument, but it was unlike any he had ever seen. It had twin

horns winding around like serpents and a long neck with strings stretched tightly across it.

"This belonged to a minstrel," said the elf. "I'm told he wandered into Jabar-Loo, but he never wandered out. Traders sold it to me, but I can't get it to make a sound. Perhaps you can play it and keep the evil away."

"Play it?" said Neal, looking the splangle up and down. "It looks like you drive it!"

Eric wondered how it would help them if it were so hard to play, but he took it and slung its strap over his shoulder, anyway. "Thank you."

"Good luck to you all!" said the elf. Then he dashed back into his tower so that the *droomar* charm would remain unbroken. "*Ooo-ooo-la-looo!*" he sang.

Ooo-ooo-la-looo! Eric repeated silently.

He wanted to stay and listen.

But Keeah spoke softly in her beast's giant ear, and the tuskadons set off.

The moment the five friends journeyed under the high trees, the forest of Jabar-Loo seemed to envelop them, and the comforting song of the *droomar* towers grew distant and faded away.

Four

Enchanted Land

Daylight ebbed as the tuskadons loped into the forest. At the same time, a thick mist rose, shrouding everything. It clung to the branches and the old temple ruins that scattered the forest floor. It moved like a ghostly serpent across the ground.

They hadn't journeyed twenty minutes before Neal asked, "Are we there yet?"

"It's so foggy, who can tell?" said Julie.

"We'll find out soon enough," said Khan.

Here and there a flicker of light fell through the tangled trees, and Eric watched their shadows lengthen across the ground as they rode.

"Time is passing quickly," he said. "A day in Jabar-Loo must last only a few hours."

"I fear we'll soon be spending the night here," said Khan.

"Hold up. What's that?" asked Julie.

Keeah halted her beast, and they all stopped. Just past a field of crumbled stones stood a grassy hill as wide and tall as a building. Narrow poles of wood poked out of it, all hung with cloth.

"They look like sails," said Eric. "And masts. What is this . . . ?"

"Oh, dear! The royal ships!" cried Khan, leaping from his beast and running to the hill.

Keeah stared at the sails. "Those ships were marooned only days ago. They look as if they've been here for years!"

"The *Jaffa Wind*!" said Khan, spying a broken mast with the remains of a blue sail clinging to it. "This must be one of the enchantments the *droomar* told us about. Princess, we may fear for your parents, but at least we know they came this way."

"Then we need to keep going," said Keeah. "They are close. I can sense it."

Without delay, the tuskadons edged around the hill of ships and lumbered deeper through the trees. The day faded quickly. When evening fell again, the beasts halted. Their giant ears shot up like wings, and their heads tilted.

"They hear something," said Neal.

Just ahead, barely visible in the dying light, were the glinting waves of a river so wide its opposite bank was out of sight.

"How will we get across?" asked Julie.

"I don't think our rides will float across," said Neal, petting his tuskadon.

Eric dismounted and tried to see across the river. The waves churned and tore along swiftly. "The river's too wild, any-way. We'd never get halfway —"

"This is Jabar-Loo," a voice cackled from the darkness. "Appearances can fool you!"

The children turned and saw a little woman hobble over to them from the shadows. She looked like a barrel with feet.

"People call me Dora!" said the woman. "The city of Jabar-Loo is across this river. I can take you over." She dug into the pockets of her ragged little coat until she pulled out a tiny twig. "Come aboard my floating palace, and see what real magic is!"

She tossed the twig into the river. At once, it grew both long and wide until it resembled a small canoe. "Come, Pillow Man, you first!"

"Floating palace, eh?" Khan said. He gulped loudly, then stepped into the little boat. The instant he did, the canoe stretched and grew larger. "Oh, my! Oh, my!"

Keeah climbed into the canoe next, and both sides unfurled to form a deep hull. When Julie boarded, she found herself stepping onto a long deck.

With each new passenger, the vessel grew and grew until, when Dora herself came aboard, it was a great long boat with plenty of room, even for the tuskadons.

"A palace indeed!" said Khan.

"Let's just hope it really is a floating one," whispered Neal.

Dora pushed her foot against the bank and — *slooosh!* — the boat sped over the waves as swiftly as a motorboat.

"Excellent!" said Khan. "I like this craft."

"One adventure ends, another begins," said Dora. "But some adventures have no end."

"I guess that's true," said Eric.

"Help a friend, and he'll help you," the old woman went on. "When a door closes, climb a tree!"

Khan glanced sideways at the others. "Quite, I'm sure."

"The eyes are windows to the soul!"

Julie frowned. "Okay . . ."

"Not everything is how it appears! The right choice means everything! Music soothes the wild beast! You only succeed by trying! Some people don't like heights! Rope is useful!"

Dora stopped talking to catch her breath and mop her brow. Meanwhile, the boat bounced over the waves.

"Thanks for the cool advice, Mrs. Dora,"

said Neal. "You should totally make fortune cookies." He nudged Eric and whispered, "This lady may be old and look like a barrel, but she really knows her stuff!"

By the time the boat nestled in an inlet on the far bank, night had fallen. The air was as black and impenetrable as oil.

"You've been so kind," said Keeah.

"Well, kindness is a virtue," said Dora.

"Another good one!" said Neal.

All of a sudden, the little woman's eyes darted toward a great wall of trees that loomed nearby. She listened, then sniffed. "I smell them. I must go. And you must hide!"

With that, she leaped into her boat, pushed off again, and was gone in the mist.

"What did she mean . . . hide?" asked Khan, sniffing the air. "I have a magnificent nose, and I don't smell anything —"

That was when they heard the sound of hooves thundering through the trees.

"Never mind!" said Khan. "Attackers!"

"Tuskadons, form a circle," said Keeah.

The creatures quickly obeyed her. Everyone jumped inside the ring of tuskadons just as a terrifying wail cut through the air. "*Auurrroo — eeee!*"

Eric dropped to the ground and aimed at the trees, his fingers sparking at the darkness. "Ready to blast!"

Branches snapped, and the sound of thumping hooves exploded from the forest. Six horned beasts, armored like rhinoceroses, bounded into the clearing. It was so dark that they would have been invisible but for the glow of golden medallions that dangled from their necks like cowbells.

"Beasts with jewelry!" yelled Neal. "Run!"

But he couldn't run. None of them could. There was no place to go. Two beasts leaped over the tuskadons at Khan and Keeah.

They knocked them together and tossed them head over heels into Julie. All three friends sprawled in a heap.

"I've got it!" said Eric. He sent a sizzling blast of silver sparks and struck the beasts' horns. They howled and dispersed. "Ha! I don't think you'll come back for more!"

But they did come back. *For* more and *with* more. When the frightening creatures returned, there were twenty of them.

"Let's take it up a notch — Keeah!" said Eric. The princess joined him, and together they sent blast after blast at the beasts. The creatures thrashed about, scattering the tuskadons.

A shaft of light tumbled down through the trees, and the air brightened suddenly.

"It's morning already!" said Julie. "We'll be able to see our attackers —"

But no sooner had the light come than the beasts wailed wildly. In the blink of an eye they galloped away through the trees and were gone.

For a few moments, the little band stood in shock, saying nothing. In those same moments, dawn rolled across the forest clearing.

"Not that I'm complaining," said Neal, his turban drooping, "but where did those ugly things go? And where are our tuskadons?"

"Gone," said Khan. "They left us with nothing."

Eric picked up the splangle from the ground, where it had fallen. "Nearly nothing. We still have this. It seems nobody wants it."

Now that daylight had come, where before they had seen only the impenetrable forest, they now saw a wall looming over them from behind the trees.

Two giant rat heads, fanged and glaring at them, surmounted a gate in the wall.

"Those rats are images from Goll," said Keeah softly. "Their temples and cities all had rat gates. To warn visitors to stay away."

Towering up into the mist beyond the wall was a great stone pyramid.

"Oh, dear," gasped Khan. "They liked to build things big in old Goll, didn't they?"

A pack of blue-furred rodents scrambling under the wall saw the children, chattered, then scurried through a tiny hole in the gate.

"They have real rats, too," said Julie.

"Jabar-Loo may be full of rats and enchantments," said Keeah, "but this is the gate, and we need to enter."

Together the five friends approached the wall, then halted. An inscription was carved in the stone over the massive gate.

Everyone turned to Eric.

"Not that we really want to know," said

Julie, "but I don't suppose you can read that?"

Eric liked knowing old Droon languages, but he didn't like knowing what these words meant. He read them aloud.

"*Alanath-ka-Jabar-Loo. Pres-ka-fesh!*"

"Which means?" asked Khan.

"Behold Jabar-Loo. Enter if you dare!"

Five

Mr. Duppy Makes a Deal

Staring up at the inscription, Neal took a step back. "Maybe we should think about this. Do we really dare to enter here? I mean, a Goll hangout with tons of blue rats? Let's discuss."

"We have to get inside," said Keeah. "But we sure can't fit through the rodent hole, and I don't suppose we can just stroll in."

"Whatever we do, splitting up is

dangerous," said Julie. "We need to stick together."

"I agree," said Khan. "Splitting is a bad idea for someone who looks like a pillow —"

"*You* there! Keep it *down*!" said a voice.

"We're trying to think," said another.

The kids spun around to see two pint-size creatures in brown cloaks and hats camping in a hollow under a tree.

"Sorry," said Keeah, with a little bow.

"Wait!" the first one said, jumping to his feet. "Is you a *princess*?" He smoothed his whiskers and hustled over, extending his paw to them. "My name's Mr. *Duppy*. Me and Mr. *Beffle* here buy and *sell* things. Anything. *Every*thing."

"And all that's in between," his friend said, extending his paw, too.

Eric wondered if they were the same

traders who had sold the splangle to the *droomar*.

"Nice to meet you," he said.

Keeah pointed to the walled city. "By any chance do you trade . . . in there?"

"All the time," said Mr. Beffle. "Prince Umberto runs the place, you see. It pays to be on his, er, friendly side."

"No matter how *tiny* that side is!" said Mr. Duppy with a laugh like a gargle.

"Prince Umberto?" said Julie.

"He's the *man*," said Mr. Duppy. "In fact, we've got an *appointment* with him *now*. So if you'll *excuse* us!"

The traders waddled back to their ditch.

Keeah looked up at the wall. "How much do you want to bet that Prince Umberto is the one who has my parents locked up?"

"And Galen and Max, too," said Neal.

"No bets," grumbled Khan. "I can sniff him already. He's why no one returns from

Jabar-Loo. It must have been his beasts that attacked us. That pretty *droomar* song is trying to stop his enchantments, I just know it!"

Eric glanced back at the traders. They had already packed up their little camp and were heading for the gate. "If only we had something to trade. But we lost everything to those creepy beasts by the river."

"Not everything," said Neal. He tapped the splangle on Eric's back. "We have this."

Eric laughed. "Except that it won't play a note. Who would want a splan —"

"Hold on!" called Mr. Duppy, his eyes widening. "Is that *the* one-of-a-kind, genuine *splangle*? Mr. Beffle, lookee!"

Grinning, Neal slid the splangle from Eric's back and trotted over to the traders, while the others scanned the high walls.

"I could fly us into the trees," said Julie, frowning at the branches that hung near the wall. "But there might be guards. . . ."

Khan wrinkled his nose. "Umberto has guards, no doubt! Evil princes always do!"

A sudden lilt of laughter erupted behind them, and they saw the traders taking the splangle from Neal and shaking his hand.

Neal raced back to his friends. "I'm so good at this! They're taking the splangle inside Jabar-Loo!"

"The splangle?" said Keeah. "But *we* need to get inside. Did you get us in?"

Neal wagged his head. "Sort of."

"Sort of?" said Julie. "What did you do?"

"I sold them Eric," he said.

Eric blinked. "What are you talking about?"

"They only wanted the splangle, which didn't help us," said Neal. "But when I said you could play it, they bought you, too." He held up a coin. "I think it's a Droon dollar."

"It's a nickel," said Keeah.

Eric glared at the coin. "You *sold* me? For a *nickel*?"

"Sure," said Neal. "When we were in the song tower, the *droomar* said you sang good. You're a natural musician, Eric."

"But you can't *sell* me!" cried Eric. "*Plus*, no one can even *play* the splangle! The only guy who *could* play it was never *seen* again!"

"You sound like my friend Mr. Duppy," said Neal. "Besides, if no one can play it, no one will know when you play it wrong. Eric, you're getting through the gate!"

"Are you nuts? *I can't play the thing!*"

"Eric, wait," said Keeah, standing between the two friends. "Maybe Neal's right. One of us inside is better than none. Once you're in, you can find a way to get us all inside."

"Besides," said Julie, "Mrs. Khan said

few travelers find Jabar-Loo, but fewer enter. You're going to enter. That's pretty special."

Special. There was that word again.

Could Jabar-Loo be part of his mystery vision, after all? Could getting inside be the only way to find out the truth?

Eric looked at the walls, then at the traders, then at his friends. "Well, I guess, maybe, but I still can't play it —"

"Time's up, Smiley!"

A hand gripped Eric and spun him around. Mr. Beffle was cradling the splangle, while Mr. Duppy held out a chain and handcuffs.

"What are those for?" asked Eric.

"You to wear," said Mr. Duppy. He clamped the cuffs on Eric's wrists and gave them a tug. "Prince Umberto's going to love you!"

As the traders pulled Eric toward the

big gate, he looked back at his friends. "But what about not splitting up? You said we shouldn't split up!"

"Oh, you'll be *split*," said Mr. Duppy with a laugh. "If Umberto doesn't like the way you *play*, you'll be split by *Glok*!"

"Glok?" said Keeah. "Who is . . . Glok?"

"Big monster. Lots of legs," said Mr. Beffle. He banged on the gate, and it slowly swung open as if on command.

"Uh, maybe I did a bad thing," said Neal.

"You think?" said Julie.

Before Eric knew it — *fooom!* — the giant gate to Jabar-Loo slammed shut behind him with a sound like thunder.

As the two traders tugged him toward the great white pyramid, he wondered how in the world he was ever going to get out of this mess.

Six

Sing for the King!

The inside of Jabar-Loo was like nothing Eric had ever seen before. Amid the crumbled ruins of old temples that lay scattered within the walls were buildings as new as the big pyramid that rose in the distance.

Something really has woken up here, Eric thought. *But what, or ... who ... could it be?*

He felt afraid at first, then sensed his

wizard power surging in his veins and knew he could break free if he had to.

He decided to go with the traders all the way to the palace. It might be the only way to find his missing friends.

The streets from the wall to the palace twisted and turned like a maze. As they passed through them, Eric saw not a single soul anywhere. "Where is everybody?"

"Sleeping late," said Mr. Beffle curtly.

"Oh, but it *is* nice to have this *splangle* again!" said Mr. Duppy. "Sold it for a *droomar* kettle once. Let's sell it for *cash* this time, eh?"

"We'll be heroes, we will," said Mr. Beffle as they zigzagged down a street. "Jabar-Loo hasn't heard music since, well, you know."

"Oh, I *know*," said Mr. Duppy. "But this boy will turn out better than *him*, I'm sure."

Eric felt his heart skip. "Better than who?"

The two traders shared a look.

"Better than the *Amazing* Flemky, of course," said Mr. Duppy. "*Poor* little fellow."

"Poor little fellow?" said Eric. "What happened to him?"

Mr. Beffle mumbled to himself, then pointed up. "See for yourself."

In the center of two crossing streets stood a very tall, very skinny pole. A tiny figure sat alone at the top.

Eric thought he saw the figure wave down at him. He waved back.

"That's the Amazing Flemky?"

"Cut down in his *prime*, he was," said Mr. Duppy. "Or rather put *up* on that pole. He made Umberto *angry*. He called himself the *best* splangle player this side of *Samarindo*."

"He wasn't, though," said Mr. Beffle.

"Sadly, no," agreed Mr. Duppy. "Saying it *did* get him into the *palace*, of course."

Eric stared at the complicated instrument and gulped. "How bad was he . . . ?"

"Well, he played the wrong note, didn't he?" said Mr. Beffle. "Just one wrong note, and Umberto banished him up that pole."

"Will he ever get down?" asked Eric.

"Oh, I'm *sure* he will," said Mr. Duppy with a sigh. "Just not in his *lifetime*."

Eric closed his eyes. "Oh, brother!"

Soon they were standing at the foot of the giant pyramid. Mr. Duppy pressed a tiny button next to the doors at the base.

Errch! The doors opened into darkness. Eric followed the traders inside. The doors closed behind them with a boom.

He shivered as they passed through one empty court after another, until they finally arrived in a vast space that Eric suspected was at the center of the pyramid.

It, too, was empty.

The traders waited a few minutes in silence. Eric was about to ask what they were waiting for when the last of the sunlight vanished, and total darkness fell.

A door flew open and in stomped hundreds of armored knights with rat-shaped helmets. They carried torches and spears twice as tall as themselves. Medallions glowed around their necks — just like the beasts by the river.

"And now we *leave* you," said Mr. Duppy. "We're off to *Samarindo*. Play that *splangle* special, you hear? There's only room for *one* on Flemky's *pole*!"

Chuckling together, the two traders released Eric, took a bag of coins from one of the soldiers, and scurried back through the halls.

"Oh, man," Eric said to himself. "What has Neal gotten me into?"

While the guards were still filing in, he looked around to see if he could spot the king and queen, but did not see them.

All of a sudden, the knights clacked their spears and shouted, "Prince Umberto!"

The room blazed with even more torchlight, and Eric turned to see a giant, covered head to toe in black armor. The helmet on his head was formed exactly like the huge rat heads on the gate. On either side of him strode a monstrous gray beast. Their claws were long and razorlike. Around their necks hung glowing medallions like the others.

Though of great size and bulk, Prince Umberto moved across the floor like liquid. He stopped when he saw Eric.

Two reddish eyes flashed from the black depths inside the helmet.

"A splangle," the giant growled, his

deep voice echoing behind his iron face. "I hope you know how to play it!"

Me, too . . . Eric said to himself. "Yes, sir!" he said out loud.

Umberto sat down on a massive black throne that sat against one wall. "In my arena tomorrow, I will be crowned king. I want you to play for the event. Play me something now. . . ."

All heads in the room turned to Eric.

"Uh . . . wow . . . so soon, huh?" Eric's fingers felt like sausages when he set them on the splangle's thin strings. He tried to swallow, but found that there was nothing to swallow. He remembered Flemky sitting at the top of that pole, and he felt sick. He knew this was why he'd never performed in a talent show. It was why he didn't like to raise his hand in class. He couldn't stand people staring at him.

He moved his fingers gently.

Thwung! Ploing! Bloink!

Umberto jumped to his feet. "Do you want to join Flemky on his pole?"

"No, sir," said Eric.

"Perhaps *this* will inspire you!" said the prince. "Bring Glok the Merciless!"

"Don't go to any trouble," said Eric.

"Bring him!" boomed Umberto.

One of the giant walls slid up to reveal an iron cage. Eric nearly choked when he saw a gargantuan spider stomp out of it.

It was the most terrifying creature he had ever seen, all drooling fangs and spiky legs. Around its neck hung a gold medallion.

Umberto muttered, the medallion lit up, and the spider moved toward Eric.

It came so close that he could see the symbols on its medallion. He knew them instantly as the dark language of Goll.

He wanted to turn away, but the creature's eyes stared into his, and the words of the strange, old boat woman flew suddenly into his head.

The eyes are windows to the soul.

Eric practically screamed.

He knew those eyes!

They belonged to Max!

Max! he cried inside his head. *Is it you? Can you hear me? What happened to you? Where is Galen? What is going on here?*

"Glok, to your cage!" boomed Umberto. The medallion glowed again, and the spider hurried away.

"Boy!" said Umberto. "Tomorrow night Glok will fight an army of gladiators, and you will play. When the stars align and the moon is full I will be crowned . . . Rat King of Pesh!"

"*Om — yee — Peshhhhh!*" sang the soldiers.

Eric's blood turned to ice.

What? Pesh? PESH?

Pesh was the ancient city in the Upper World where Salamandra came from!

What did Pesh have to do with this?

What did Salamandra have to do with this?

What was going on here?!

Eric knew then that things were far more serious than he'd realized. Pesh and Jabar-Loo were connected some-how. And Salamandra was involved, too.

But how?

How?

"Better come up with a song about me," said Umberto. "Something full of rhyme."

"But I . . ."

"What did you say?" growled Umberto.

"Yes, sir!" said Eric, bowing.

"That's what I thought you said," boomed the giant. "Come, my beasts, to the little red door of my royal crown maker. Come!"

Umberto muttered words softly, and every single medallion in the room glowed.

"The medallions..." Eric said to himself. But when Umberto's two beasts glanced at him, his heart nearly burst in his chest.

In the eyes of those two beasts, he saw eyes that he knew. Umberto's hideous creatures were none other than King Zello and Queen Relna!

"No . . . no . . ." he whispered. "No!"

Eric soon found himself alone in the vast room. He couldn't believe what he had seen.

"We'll get you out of here, Max, Relna, and Zello. I promise! We can do it. I can do it. Whatever it takes, we'll get you out of here!"

Seven

Beasts of Bronze

Eric stumbled through the palace, trying to understand what he had just seen and heard.

"Umberto's controlling everyone with his medallions," he said to himself. "There are Goll symbols on the medallions, and he knows dark magic. Oh, my gosh, the king and queen! And Max! We have to save them. We have to save them!"

He reached the palace doors and slipped out. He looked both ways and hurried down a narrow passage toward the gate.

"Galen must be here, too," he whispered. "But he's probably been changed like the others."

Whatever dark power Umberto had, Eric guessed that being crowned the Rat King of Pesh would only make it worse.

Pesh!

The more he thought about that strange city, the more he thought about Salamandra — and about his vision.

Then he shook his head to clear it.

There was no time for that now.

"This way, knights!" boomed a voice.

Eric ducked behind a pile of ruined stones and spied Umberto, his twin beasts, and a dozen rat-helmeted soldiers heading for the city gate.

"So how will I get out of here now?" he muttered.

Just then, he heard a cough. "Ahem . . ."

He looked up. The Amazing Flemky waved down at him from his pole. As Eric waved back, he happened to glance from the pole to the trees outside the wall and saw that they were the same height. "Huh . . ."

Flemky coughed again. "Water! Please!"

He motioned to a bucket lying on the ground at the bottom of the pole. It was tied to a rope that dangled from the top.

At once, Eric remembered something else the boat woman Dora had said.

Help a friend, and he'll help you!

"Of course!" he said to himself. Keeping out of sight of Umberto and his men, Eric ran to the pole and unhooked the bucket. He found a shallow pool of rainwater in the street, filled the bucket, then tied it back on the rope. He scribbled a note and tied that on, too, then gave Flemky the thumbs-up.

Flemky pulled the bucket to the top.

A few moments later, Eric saw him read the note, then return the thumbs-up sign.

This time the rope descended without the bucket. When Eric grabbed hold, the rope began to rise. With one eye on Umberto, Eric pushed against the pole and began to swing. The farther he swung, the higher he flew, until he was nearly as high as the trees.

On one final swing, Eric soared up and reached out to the branches. He caught one! It bounced under his weight, but he clung tight. He was in a tree!

"Thanks, Flemky!" he whispered. Tying the rope to the branch, he edged in to the trunk and lowered himself inch by inch until there was one branch left.

"I can't believe I made it!" he said.

He spoke too soon. The branch snapped under him and he plummeted to the ground. "*Ahhhhhh!*"

"*Ahhh*, yourself!" said a tiny voice under him.

Eric jumped to his feet only to find Khan, the Lumpy king, lying flat on his back in the dirt.

"Soft landing, was it?" Khan groaned. "You nearly knocked the stuffing clear out of me!"

Eric helped him up. "Khan, I'm so sorry!"

The king fluffed his shoulders. "Well, at least you're all right. Everyone, look!"

"Eric, we were so worried," said Julie, running out of the forest with the others.

"We waited as long as we could, then went to hide," said Keeah. "I'm glad you're safe."

"Thanks," said Eric. "But none of us is safe. And we're about to be less safe still. Umberto is nearly here. Hide!"

The friends piled up the tree Eric had fallen from just as the city gates swung open. The soldiers, beasts, and Umberto marched through, leading the band of blue rats the kids had seen before.

"Umberto is that creepy giant with the rat helmet," Eric whispered. "He transforms people with those medallions. They have symbols from ancient Goll all over them. I didn't see Galen, but Umberto turned Max into the monster Glok. And Keeah . . ."

She gasped. "My parents! You saw them. They're in danger. I know it —"

Eric shook his head. "I'm not sure. In fact, I don't think they are in actual danger.

Umberto has enchanted them, too, and now . . . well, you see those two beasty things?"

"Oh, no!" Keeah gasped. "My parents?"

"But I think they're okay for now," Eric said quickly. "Because he's controlling them, they're on his side —"

"Hush!" said Khan. "Look there!"

Umberto lowered a medallion over the head of each tiny rodent. Then he spread his massive arms wide and spoke.

"What's he doing?" asked Julie.

"You'll see," said Eric.

At once, the medallions glowed, and with a terrifying roar the blue rats transformed into the giant beasts the kids had seen at the river. They stomped and snorted, then bowed before the prince as if waiting for his command.

"Destroy the song towers!" Umberto bellowed. "Soon I shall be the Rat King, and the time for Jabar-Loo to rise will come! Destroy the towers!"

Wailing as before, the beasts thundered away into the night. In a flash, Umberto and the others reentered the gate. It closed with a resounding boom.

Keeah looked at the gate, then turned to the forest. "As much as it hurts me to say it, my parents can wait. The *droomar* are not a fighting people. We have to stop those beasts, and we have to stop them at the river."

Eric's fingers sparked. "Let's do it!"

Keeah conjured a coil of spinning blue light. Before they knew it, the children and Khan were zooming toward the raging river.

It was the middle of the night and pitch black when they alighted on the near bank. The rapids splashed along in the darkness.

"This is the narrowest part of the river," said Keeah. "They'll try to cross here."

No sooner had they scrambled into position, than the monstrous beasts exploded through the trees, wailing at the top of their lungs.

Eric aimed his fingers and sent a stream of hot sparks at the beasts.

The first two beasts avoided the blast and charged away, but the second two fell into each other. The two remaining creatures drew up short behind them.

"Pull back," said Eric as the beasts regrouped. "Don't let them near the river!"

"I hate fighting in the dark," said Neal. "I can't see where to hide!"

All of a sudden, branches snapped behind them and the barrel-shaped boat woman tumbled out of the underbrush.

"Can I help?" Dora cackled.

"Uh . . . yes!" said Julie. "Thanks!"

"You do seem to need it!" Dora said. "Here, pull a thread from my sleeve!"

They did as she said, but what came from her sleeve was not thread but rope as thick as ship's rigging.

"Now weave a web among the trees!" she said. "We can hold them off until dawn!"

While the beasts assembled for a second assault, the children, Khan, and Dora rigged the rope to and fro among the trees.

"Get ready to pull!" said Dora. "Now!"

When the creatures charged, the children pulled the rope tightly. It flew up and tangled the beasts' hooves, sending them crashing to the ground. The beasts staggered up, but the children pulled the rope tight a second time, and the creatures stumbled again. They repeated this action over

and over, until a glimmer of light finally appeared in the eastern sky.

"Dawn!" cried Dora. "Beasts, go home to your evil master. The light of day has come!"

As if they understood the dreaded word *day*, the armored beasts wailed loudly and galloped back through the trees to Jabar-Loo.

The riverbank was quiet once more.

"We actually stopped them!" said Julie.

"Yay!" yelled Neal. "Thank you, boat lady!"

But when they turned to where the little woman had been standing, they saw no one. Dora had vanished into the mist.

"That lady comes and goes really fast," said Eric. "But she's helped us a lot so far."

"A new friend, perhaps?" said Khan.

"But come, we have some old friends to save!"

By the time the little band arrived at Jabar-Loo, the beasts were no more, and the last of the blue rats were scurrying through the hole in the city wall.

Eric looked up. The sun was moving quickly across the sky. "Max's battle with the gladiators starts soon."

"How do we get inside?" asked Julie.

Eric pointed to the trees. "By going up."

One by one, the friends climbed the giant tree into Jabar-Loo. As they did, Eric kept turning two things over in his mind.

The first was . . . how were they ever going to fight the old dark magic of Goll?

The second was . . . what rhymes with Umberto?

Eight

Behind the Little Red Door

Eric reached the top branch first and untied Flemky's rope. He waved to the little creature on top of the pole.

"Who is that?" asked Keeah.

Eric smiled. "The wandering splangle player the *droomar* told us about. He's another new friend. We'll have to free him, too."

"The list grows," said Neal. "Cool."

By the time the little band had swung

down and landed in the street, it was midday.

"Okay," said Eric, peering both ways before he headed down a deserted alley. "Umberto is bad now, but he'll be lots worse when he's crowned Rat King."

Neal pulled his turban lower. "Not to mention probably creepier to look at."

"We have to wreck that crown," said Julie.

"Exactly," said Eric. "It's made by a jeweler behind a red door. Let's look for a red door."

Keeah nodded. "To the palace!"

The five friends wormed their way through the empty streets and into the palace. They searched every deserted hallway until they spied a small red door.

"Here we are," whispered Keeah. "If all the baddies come out only at night, it's probably empty. Let's take a look inside —"

Just as they were going to enter, they heard the sound of a hammer tapping — *plinka-tap-tap!* — and the faint buzz of someone humming — "*Mmm . . . mm-mmm-mmm!*"

Neal pressed his ear to the door. "No way! I know that sound. But it can't be!"

"My goodness, never!" whispered Khan.

One by one, they recognized the tapping of that hammer and the humming of that tune.

Hob is busy hammering
Crowns and medals for the king —

"Hob?" whispered Keeah. "Hob! That furry little imp? He made mischief once after being in Jabar-Loo. Could he be here again? As Umberto's crown maker?"

Eric shivered. *It all makes sense. Hob. Pesh. Salamandra really is involved in this!*

He couldn't help himself. He jumped through the door and tumbled into Hob's workshop. "We've found you at last!"

The scruffy little imp fell off his stool. "Ahh! Who surprises Hob at his important work?"

"Important work? More like evil work!" said Keeah. "Hob, what are you doing here?"

The imp dropped his hammer, lowered his head, and grew sullen. "Nothing . . ."

"Not nothing!" said Khan. "Working for that Prince Umberto, you mean —"

"Umberto!" Hob slumped to the floor. "That spirit of darkness! Umberto is forcing Hob to make this evil rat crown!"

The imp touched the great black crown on the workbench. Like Umberto's helmet, it bore the image of a rat's head. The symbols of Goll were carved all over it.

Keeah stood over Hob. "Tell us what's

going on here. What happened to my parents? And who *is* Umberto?"

The imp wept into his hands. "Since you last saw Hob, he has wandered many miles across Droon, Salamandra's thorn staff by his side. By and by he came to Jabar-Loo, seeking magic to make a perfect, living mask!"

"My impish little friend," said Khan, "dark magic frees no one."

"Hob has learned exactly that!" said the mask maker. "Umberto was a . . . *being* who long ago sought to conquer the ancient city of Pesh in the Upper World. Salamandra banished him to the Underworld. The Underworld? Ha! Umberto found his way to Droon! For long years after his defeat, he was a mere shadow. He needed powerful magic to return. He needed a powerful form. Silly Hob gave him both!"

"How?" asked Eric.

"By the time Hob blundered into Umberto's lair amid the ruins of Goll," said the imp, "Umberto had soaked up Goll's ancient magic. The old, dark ways lived in him! He stole Hob's magic staff. Then he forced Hob to make a giant suit of armor he could live inside and medallions for thousands of jungle rats. Once he dons this crown of ultimate power, no longer will night be his only time to live. His control over the rats will be complete, and he will leave Jabar-Loo to invade the rest of Droon. The king and queen are already slaves to him. He has transformed your royal navy —"

Keeah gasped. "The navy! Where are they?"

Hob shrank. "Umberto's gladiators! He will pit them against the spider troll tonight! Everyone in his power will suffer!"

"Even Flemky?" asked Julie.

"Except Flemky," said Hob. "Hob doesn't like heights. He wouldn't go up that pole to put the medallion on him."

"What does Jabar-Loo have to do with Pesh?" asked Eric. "And how could Salamandra banish Umberto from Pesh to Droon? They're in two different worlds."

"Ahhhh," Hob sighed. "There are connections between the worlds even Hob has not discovered!"

Eric stared at the imp. *Connections?*

"Why don't we just destroy the crown?" asked Julie. She reached for the crown, but it zapped her suddenly, hurling her back into Neal. "Oww!" she said. "Never mind."

"It's a Hob crown," said the imp with a grin. "It's indestructible by ordinary magic!"

"Nothing is easy, is it?" asked Neal.

"Neither easy nor hopeful," said Hob, trembling. "Oh, Hob is so very afraid!"

Eric looked at his friends one by one. They had nothing but fear in their faces.

And why not?

Galen was nowhere to be found. Max was a monster. The king and queen were under Umberto's control. His rat army was enormous. Eric felt his knees go weak and his blood turn to ice.

At the same time, he knew that they would have to do something. That *he* would have to do something.

"People, we need to be there when Umberto crowns himself Rat King," he said. "The arena is where we'll stop him."

"Stop him? Stop him?" Hob's whiskers twitched nervously. "Umberto will use Hob's magic staff to make certain he becomes king!"

Eric tried not to show how afraid he was. "Hob, we need more medallions, ones to make us *look* like the other gladiators, but not be under Umberto's control. Can you do that?"

Keeah looked at Eric. "You've got something special in mind, haven't you?"

Eric's heart skipped a beat when he heard that word. "It'll be special . . . if it works. We need to be in that arena. But only make four medallions. I won't need one. I have to play the splangle."

"Make three medallions," said Keeah. "I'm going with Eric. I've got to be near my parents, and no disguise is getting in my way."

Eric was glad a friend would be with him. "Thanks. I could use the help."

"Hob is still very fearful!" said the imp.

"Don't forget, my little friend," said

Khan. "Eric and Keeah will be in that arena right next to you!"

Eric glanced at Umberto's terrifying crown. It was sparking wildly. "Something tells me that will be the most dangerous place of all."

Nine

Rat King

Hob's tapping and banging ceased with the blare of a trumpet. Night had fallen.

"Your medallions are finished," the imp said. "These will change your shape, but you will be subject to your own wills, not Umberto's."

"Just don't be afraid when you see me as a fierce gladiator," said Neal. "It'll still be me under all that armor."

Eric grinned. "I'll try to remember."

Hob searched the children's faces. His own was pale and frightened. "When the moon is overhead and the stars align in the shape of a V, Umberto will remove his helmet and don this crown. For a moment, you will see his terrifying shadow self. Princess, that is your only chance to remove your parents' medallions. If you fail, they will be Umberto's slaves forever!"

Keeah nodded grimly. "I understand."

Hob looked at Neal, Julie, and Khan. "In that same moment you will have a chance to free Max. Finally, Eric, you can destroy the crown then and only then. You will need special magic to do that. If he lowers it upon his hideous head, it can never be removed."

Eric made a face. "No pressure."

All at once, Hob stiffened and placed the rat crown on a pillow. He moved toward the door as if in a trance. "Umberto calls. Hob goes. . . . Hob goes. . . ."

As the mask maker left, Neal, Julie, and Khan put on the medallions he had crafted. At first, Eric and Keeah gasped as they watched their friends change.

Then they laughed

Instead of becoming giant gray-armored knights, the three friends began to shrink. When they finally stopped, they looked like a trio of kindergartners armed with ice-cream spoons.

"What's this?" Neal squeaked in a high voice, waving his spoon around. "I thought we were going to be giants with amazing swords!"

Eric and Keeah were still giggling, but they stopped short. It suddenly became clear what had happened.

"The gladiators are tiny!" he said.

"Umberto wants them small, so that Glok will destroy them!" said Keeah. "So that . . . Max will destroy them!"

"Change us back!" squealed Khan. "I don't want to be any smaller than I really am!"

Eric breathed in. "But we all need to be in the arena. Umberto can't know you're there. Please, just go find the other gladiators and try to blend in. We'll be with Umberto and Hob. Come on, people, we can do this!"

With a quick nod, Julie scurried through the doorway. Khan and Neal tried to catch up.

Eric shared a look with Keeah. "Oh, this will be fun. Or not."

"I can't wait," she said. "Come on."

When the two friends reached the arena, they found a vast open area surrounded by stone seats that rose to a dizzying height. In the seats were thousands of rat-helmeted soldiers. Their medallions glinted in the torchlight. Their eyes flashed menacingly through the slits in their helmets.

"There are so many of them!" said Eric.

When the gladiators marched in, the kids saw that the royal navy of Droon had indeed been transformed into tiny, spoon-wielding warriors. Neal, Khan, and Julie were near the front.

"Man, this is bad for us. . . ." said Eric.

"This is bad for everyone," said Keeah, glancing at the night sky. "Come on. Hurry."

They headed up the stands to the summit where Umberto stood, larger than life. Hob stood entranced next to him, the crown on a pillow in his hands. Umberto pointed the magic staff at Keeah.

"Who is *she*?" he demanded angrily.

"My official splangle tuner?" said Eric.

"See that she does a good job!" Umberto snorted. Right behind him sat Keeah's parents, growling.

Umberto thudded his staff once, and the arena went silent. "My loyal army! I have waited centuries to come into my own again. This little mask maker has made it possible! When midnight comes, the Rat King of Pesh shall rise! We shall leave Jabar-Loo and conquer Droon!"

Umberto's army exploded in cheers. Eric shuddered to see their terrifying eyes. He glanced back at the twin beasts that were Keeah's parents. He looked at the doomed gladiators below. The whole scene terrified him. He knew he had only seconds to stop Umberto's crowning. He hoped he was up to the challenge.

"Let the games begin!" Umberto howled. "Release Glok!"

Errrck! An iron gate rose below the stands.

Glok was more terrifying than Eric remembered. It had grown. Its eight legs were now twenty. Its feelers snapped angrily in the air. It glared at the tiny gladiators and drooled.

"Gladiators, advance!" shouted Umberto.

Neal, Julie, Khan, Eric spoke silently to his friends, *look fierce and go to Max, but don't hurt him or let him hurt you!*

As soon as Neal, Khan, and Julie pushed their way to the front of the gladiators, the giant spider shrieked and hissed.

The three friends scurried first one way, then another. Max/Glok leaped here and there, trying to catch them. Every few seconds Eric glanced up at the sky. The moon, not yet overhead, was rising quickly. Five bright stars were moving into alignment.

But things were going bad quickly for

the three gladiators. Neal tripped on his own feet and tumbled to the ground right in front of Max. When Khan and Julie scurried to help him up, Max closed in on them, too.

In seconds, all three friends were trapped. The soldiers in the arena roared wildly.

Poised above Neal, Julie, and Khan, the giant spider turned its head toward Umberto. Its pincerlike claws were raised to strike.

"Glok, my wild beast!" boomed Umberto.

Suddenly, Eric remembered another of Dora's sayings. *Music soothes the wild beast.*

"Music soothes the wild beast?" he said. He glanced down at his splangle. "Umberto, I need to play a song first! I need to!"

Eric knew he couldn't play the splangle.

He couldn't play a note. But he had to do something to stall for time.

"I have a song," he said. "I really do —"

"Too late!" growled Umberto. "Glok, destroy the gladiators!"

The spider wailed and raised himself high over the three friends, prepared to lunge.

"What? Noooo!" cried Eric. Without thinking, he raced down the stands, the splangle still in his hands. He didn't know what he was going to do, but he had to try to save his friends. He charged across the arena to Max. "Stop! Stop! Stop!"

At that moment, a silvery light shone down from above.

The stars were aligned in a perfect V, and the bright full moon stood in their center.

It was midnight.

"No, no, no . . ." Eric gasped.

"Behold the Rat King of Pesh!" Umberto wailed. "Droon's next ruler!"

The arena thundered with the sound of thousands of armored soldiers rising to their feet. They wailed like demons inside their rat-faced helmets.

"Droon — is — ours!" they cried.

With one iron hand clutching the magic staff, Umberto removed the dreadful mask from his head. Where his face should have been whirled a horrifying cloud of black air. He snatched the rat crown from Hob.

"Eric!" Keeah cried, running to her parents.

Amid spraying sparks and roaring wind, Umberto lowered the rat crown onto his head.

Ten

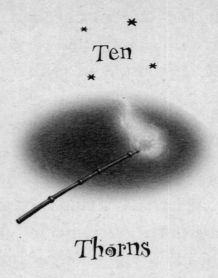

Thorns

When Umberto lowered the crown, ragged black air coiled around his entire body like wings of darkness. Shadows dripped like liquid fire from the crown, oozing over his shoulders and forming a scaly skin of shimmering black.

Shadows ran down his arms and side, staining them in garments the color of night.

"Droon — is — ours!" yelled the Rat King.

"*Om — yee — Pesh!*" replied his army.

Eric cried out as he saw Keeah's parents leap angrily at her.

He whirled around to see the terrifying giant spider — Max! — lunging at his friends.

"NOOOOOO!" he screamed. He took the splangle and slammed it against the ground in rage. "NOOOOOO!"

All at once, the instrument sounded.

Bring-aling-aling!

The sound was clear and soft and sweet. And yet as soft as it was, the sound echoed through the air like a large, shimmering bird.

And everything stopped.

The spider halted in mid-leap. Umberto's twin beasts were caught in the air before they reached Keeah. The soldiers, the gladiators, even the Rat King himself slowed and slowed and slowed until they ceased to move.

Everything froze, stilled, stopped.

Everything was silent.

Nothing moved.

Nothing. Except Eric.

And except the magic staff. It flew out of Umberto's iron hand and its tangle of thorns burst into flames.

The staff whirled across the whole length of the arena. Astonished, Eric followed it with his eyes until it stopped in the hand of someone he knew.

"Thank you, Eric. I've been wanting this!"

Dora, the old boat woman, hobbled toward him, holding the staff in her hands.

With every step she took, however, she changed. Her old rags melted away, and in their place appeared a cloak of brilliant green.

"Salamandra!" said Eric. "It was you!"

She smiled. "Here I am. And here you are."

When she stopped in front of Eric, the fragrance of fresh apples fell over him.

He knew Salamandra had come from the ancient past of his world. In a way, she was still a teenager, but she seemed older than before. Wiser, perhaps. More weary. But a glimmer of mischief still haunted her features. Her dark lips smiled as if she heard his silent thoughts.

"I have lived five thousand years," she said. "My wandering has aged me, wearied me. I needed your help to regain my magic staff."

"You needed our help?" said Eric. "But you helped us from the beginning! You gave us clues. 'Rope is fun. Music soothes the beast.' You helped us all the way. Why?"

"Without my staff, I couldn't hope to defeat Umberto. I needed you and your friends," she said.

"You *knew* this would happen," he said.

"I came from the future. I saw . . . *some* things," she said. "Things about you, too. Some good, some not. Special things. You'll really be special now, Eric Hinkle."

A shiver went up his neck. *How . . . ?*

Salamandra cast a glance at Umberto. Her features grew frosty. "Only you have the power to stop the Rat King."

"What? No! It's too late!" Eric felt a lump in his throat grow and thicken. "Maybe I had the power. For a few seconds. But I didn't do anything. I was so lame. I ran to my friends when I should have been trying to destroy the crown. It's too late. The Rat King exists!"

Salamandra moved the staff toward him as if to light his face by its blazing tangle of thorns. "In different ways, you and I, Eric, are necessary for the future of Droon. But the cost will be high. You have a price to pay, if you choose to."

He almost wasn't listening. Looking over the scene around him, he felt like crying. It had gone so wrong. *Special? I don't think so!*

"We're all paying a price today," he said.

She looked into his eyes. "If you take my staff, you can change all this. Our powers joined together, working together, can change this. There is still time to do what you must. The choice is yours."

"Our powers? Working together?" he said.

She smiled and nodded.

Trembling, Eric took the staff from her. When he did, he felt immense power flow between himself and the staff.

"What choice do I have to make?" he asked.

"Oh, you've already made it!"

With that, Salamandra was gone in a puff of green smoke, and time came rushing back in a blur of movement around him.

"Gladiators, advance!" shouted a voice.

Eric was shocked to see Umberto high in the stands, not yet transformed into the hideous Rat King.

"What's going on?" he cried. Looking up, he saw the stars not yet in alignment and the moon still moving toward them.

"I went back in time!" he whispered.

"Salamandra sent me back in time! I can change things! I can fix them!"

"Glok, my wild beast!" boomed Umberto.

Eric smiled when he saw the thorn staff in his hands.

"Umberto!" he yelled. "I was going to play a song. Instead, I think I'll just knock your head off!"

Eric rushed up the stands as quickly as his legs could carry him. He reached Umberto just as the bright moon burst over the arena. The moment had arrived.

"Behold the Rat King of Pesh!" Umberto wailed. "Droon's next —!"

"Oh, can it, Fog Face!" cried Eric.

With a single swing of the powerful thorn staff, he struck the rat crown just as Umberto tried to lower it onto his head.

Wha-boooom! The crown blew apart

into a thousand fragments of black iron and gold.

The sound was a tremendous earth-rending crack of thunder that tore the air in two.

Eric staggered and fell, barely conscious. Umberto himself collapsed on the stones in a heap of broken armor. His shadow oozed away from the fragments. It formed a coil of ragged black smoke, shot into the sky, and vanished. Simply vanished. The moment he did, the sun rose over the horizon.

Eric wobbled to his feet. "He's gone! Salamandra did it! *We* did it. Umberto's gone!"

At once, medallions clattered to the ground all across the arena, and the soldiers were nowhere to be seen. All that remained were thousands of rats. They scurried away in fright.

Glok's medallion fell to the sand — *clink* — and the giant spider melted away. Max stood in its place, as small, orange-haired, and chirpy as ever.

The medallions fell from Umberto's twin beasts, and Keeah's parents stood in their place. With cries of joy, they embraced their daughter.

The sailors of the Droon navy were restored as well. Neal, Khan, and Julie ran up the stands, back to their normal selves again, too.

The friends all hugged one another for a long time, until a familiar voice called them.

"Everyone, hello there!"

They turned. Galen the wizard, in full cloak and hat, stood in the arena, smiling broadly.

"Where have you been?" asked Keeah, rushing to his side.

Galen smiled. "Looking down on you all from a great height." He turned and pointed back toward Flemky's pole. The top was empty.

"Galen was Flemky?" gasped Neal.

"And Flemky was Galen?" said Khan.

"Just as the splangle is nothing but my staff!" said Galen. He thrust out his hand, and the fragments of the broken splangle collected in his hand. They stretched and narrowed into his long staff once more.

"I met Salamandra outside the gate," he told them. "She told me what was going on inside Jabar-Loo and that you were coming. Sometimes, you must trust, even when you doubt. So I played my part and helped where I could. Salamandra hinted that you all would stop Umberto." He turned to Eric. "And you did!"

Eric breathed in. "She told me things. About the future. About me."

Queen Relna put her arm on his shoulder. "Truth can be found in the most mysterious places and from the most mysterious people," she said. "And Salamandra may very well know what lies in wait for all of us."

"Let's not forget she is a riddler," said Max, fluffing his hair. He seemed glad to be himself again. "I, for one, am not sure whether I shall ever trust her."

Eric wondered whether he would, either. She spoke in riddles he often couldn't understand. But he remembered that moment when he held her staff and felt power move between him and it. Something happened in that moment. He quietly flicked his own fingers twice and realized she had told him the truth. There had been a price to pay.

"Oh, *hey* there!" shouted a voice.

They all turned to see Mr. Duppy and Mr. Beffle waddle into the arena, chuckling.

"Wait for it," said Neal. "In a few seconds, they'll change."

Everyone stood back, waiting for the two traders to transform into something else.

They didn't.

"Awkward *silence* there," said Mr. Duppy. "Anyway, we'd like to *trade* for *these*, if we may!" He whistled, and several big creatures entered the arena.

"Our tuskadons!" said Julie.

"Traveling on these fellows would cut our time to Samarindo in half," said Mr. Beffle.

"The tuskadons are friends of the *droomar*," said Keeah. "Maybe you can work out a deal with them."

"Well, then," said Mr. Duppy, "we'll

just be *off*!" He and Mr. Beffle led the tuskadons out.

"So, they were just themselves?" asked Neal.

Galen laughed. "Sometimes things really *are* what they seem!"

"Uh, Hob is gone again," said Max, looking all around. The scruffy imp was nowhere to be seen.

"And sometimes," said Galen, still laughing, "some *things* are just as they should be."

"Before that changes again," said King Zello, "I suggest we all go home!"

Together, the king, the queen, the children, Galen, Khan, Max, and the entire Droon navy marched out of Jabar-Loo toward the *droomar* song towers. When they came to the hill that had been overgrown, they found the ships restored and moored in an inlet of the sea.

A breeze lifted the sails of the navy's ships, and they bobbed brightly on the water.

"The sun shines for us today," said Zello. "Perfect sailing weather. Navy, let us set off!"

The low chanting from the *droomar* song towers floated over the waves and seemed to guide the ships straight to the open seas.

Soon enough, the children spotted the rainbow staircase hovering over the water.

"Umberto's shadow is gone," said Eric. "But Salamandra is back."

"And Ko, Emperor of Beasts, is assembling his troops," added Max. "After a good night's rest, I think we'll all be busily back at work!"

"One adventure twists and turns and soon becomes another," said Queen Relna.

Eric knew that was true. Things changed all the time in Droon. He knew it already had changed for him. And he knew that among his friends, he really *was* special now.

Waving good-bye, the children raced up the stairs. Pausing midway, Eric looked down at the world of Droon he loved so much.

He flicked his fingers again and saw no sparks. He knew that his choice that day had been a real one. Whatever else had happened, one thing was sure.

His wizard powers were gone.

THE SECRETS OF DROON

By Tony Abbott

Read them all!

Under the stairs, a magical world awaits you!

SCHOLASTIC

www.scholastic.com/droon

SODBL05

WITHDRAWN